I0607992

Susan: The Naughty Innocent

Dorian Shellan

Published by Haines Communications, 2024.

SUSAN: THE NAUGHTY INNOCENT

First edition. February 5, 2024.

ISBN: 978-1637860380

Written by Dorian Shellan.

Table of Contents

Susan: The Naughty Innocent
by Dorian Shellan

Chapter One: Susan

Natalie was only eighteen years old when first married, and she gave birth to a daughter, Susan, less than a year later. It was a happy marriage, but her husband, ever pursuing wealth and feeling invincible, was killed while on a speculative trip to the gold fields of Africa fifteen years later. When she learned she was destitute, Natalie eagerly accepted a marriage proposal from, Sir Eustace Smithers, a family friend whose wife had recently died. The fact that Sir Eustace was very wealthy more than compensated for his being more than twelve years her senior. Furthermore, his age did not deter him from carnal pleasures. He possessed a large stiff cock with which he would poke her not infrequently and in a masterful fashion, a mode that Natalie most enjoyed. He also enjoyed birching her for his pleasure as well as requiring her to service him with her mouth, and occasionally he would bind and bugger her. He was in all senses, so far as Natalie was concerned, a most amorous gentleman, vigorous and soldierly in manner, who extolled from his wife such pleasures as he wished in return for keeping her in more than mere comfort. Laden with many private treasures as she had been, mostly in the form of necklaces, rings, and other expensive trinkets, Natalie forgave him all, even to the extent of aiding his caprices with several of the younger female servants, who came and went as fast as raindrops.

"I will have her, my dear, this evening," Sir Eustace would say languidly at dinner, indicating some fresh young girl who had come under his eye when brought into their service.

"Yes, my dear," Natalie would answer, and would feel quite an amorous shiver run through her at the thought of her lord and master putting his manly cock to the girl. She might perhaps whimper and struggle until she took the pleasure of it, after which she would be slipped a sovereign or two by Natalie, who not infrequently watched the amorous battle, being satisfied when the girl was filled to the brim with her master's effusion. Watching her husband's gleaming shaft emerge from a clinging nest, Natalie would feel true pride, ever knowing that it would remain stiff for her afterwards when the maid had been dismissed.

Not only were servants served in this manner, however, as Natalie had good cause to know. There soon came a time when her husband's eyes strayed not to a new young servant but to Natalie's daughter, his stepdaughter, of whom he insisted that she call him papa. Natalie had at first pretended not to notice this, but then, being a woman of egotistical philosophy and ever mindful of the brimming coffers, she had drawn a discreet shade over her eyes, constantly reminding herself that her husband's virile tool ever sought new pastures and stayed none in long save her own.

At the age of eighteen, Susan displayed all of the physical attributes of her mother. Her breasts were full and firm, her waist was of pleasing smallness, her thighs well fleshed, and having a bottom as provocative as any demure young lady might secretly wish to possess. Susan, however, was far from being demure in her inner nature. Outwardly, she affected a prim and proper appearance, such that none would have suspected her to be a secret erotomaniac who lusted after the affection of her papa.

As to Susan's seduction, it was an artful variation of the classical mode. One that Natalie had discovered through her peering in keyholes. Her suspicions had first been slightly aroused by her husband's decision to install a comfortable divan in his study, an article of furniture that he had never previously found use for.

Apprised on the first occasion that Susan had misbehaved and must be given a taste of the strap, as Sir Eustace casually put it, Natalie had not only agreed that disciplinary measures were sometimes requisite but had herself scolded an apparently tearful Susan into attending upon her stepfather in his study. Within a minute or two of her doing so, there came to Natalie's ears the sound of the leather being regularly applied with that particular splatting, smacking sound that a good broad strap produces. Being concerned at the time with the household accounts, Natalie absorbed these background noises casually until it distantly occurred to her that her offspring was making remarkably little noise herself. This being her papa's first attendance on her bottom, Natalie naturally expected to hear loud squeals and cries, a detail evidently forgotten by Susan in her excitement. Or perhaps she simply thought that her mother was otherwise too occupied to take notice.

Natalie was never lost in the matter of fine instincts and raised her head several times to listen. Hearing then several strange moans emanating from her daughter, though muffled by distance and the closed door of the study, she became ever more curious as to the manner of Susan's reception of the strap across her bottom. Insofar as the rhythmic slapping of the leather still sounded, and seemed to be rather prolonged even for her husband, Natalie took herself along the upper corridor to her master's haven and applied her eye to the keyhole.

What she then saw was truly remarkable. Susan was indeed bending, though not as convention would have it, over her papa's desk. With her skirts and petticoat well tucked up to her hips and her frilly white drawers at her ankles, the nature of her posture was such that she was gently manipulating the well-risen prick of her papa with her right hand, while he was seated comfortably on a wooden chair beside his desk. He, for his part, was fondling her naked bottom and much else while slapping the strap idly on the leather arm of another chair.

Drawing her mouth to his, Sir Eustace then proceeded to kiss it most lusciously while that his fervent palm caressed the smooth hemispheres of Susan's cherubic bottom. Moving her legs apart as far as the banding of her drawers would permit, Susan offered herself invitingly to the lewd insinuations of his fingers, which, from moment to moment, curled right under her bottom and titillated her cunt, making her hips wriggle agreeably. Her bottom was indeed somewhat pink, but whether this was from some initial ministrations of the leather or the result of the fervent caresses it was receiving, Natalie was unable to decide. This conundrum was, however, solved for her by the murmurings of conversation that then came to her ears. "Do you not like it, my pet?"

"Oh, yes, Papa, and how big it is. Truly it became stiff the moment I pushed my drawers down. Is it not naughty for us to do this, though?"

"Indubitably, my darling, but that is the spice of it. What an adorable little slit you have, and how moist it is after your strapping."

"Wicked Papa, I thought you would not leather my poor bottom. It stung me so."

"That is its intent, my dear, to bring your bottom well up to your papa's cock, as so it did. What silky thighs you have and how plump and firm your bottom is. Rub faster, my pet. Put your tongue in my mouth and open your legs more so that I can tease you all the better."

"Ooooh, Papa." Susan cooed. "I feel so strange."

"You are about to spend, Susan, even as I. Soon enough I shall put my cock to your cunt and we will lather one another deliciously. Ah, you minx, work your bottom and tongue more."

Stung by jealousy, and yet not a little moved by the amorous spectacle, Natalie would have found herself quite unable to move had it not been for the unwanted intrusion on the upper floor of one of the servants, which caused her to hasten back to her room where she sat in a frightful lather of frustration at not knowing the continuance of the affair. As luck would have it, however, the intruding maid caused her brush and pan to drop, which in turn alarmed the overheated occupants of the study and Susan in particular. Fearing that her mama was about to witness the stolen moment, she uttered a little cry of alarm and, starting back from her papa, swiftly pulled her drawers up. He, realizing that the opportunity was lost, just as hastily covered himself and loudly proffered vocal warnings to his stepdaughter that he prayed might be heard beyond the door and so exculpate the pair.

Within minutes, while Susan hastened to her room, Sir Eustace presented himself to his wife in such a lewd state that she, deeming it better not to confess what she had witnessed, fell back upon their bed at his gruff bidding and received within seconds the lordly offering of his bubbling semen.

"My dear, what an excited state you were in," Natalie chided him softly, his throbbing prick still soaked in her well lubricated quim.

"Indeed, it must be the heat of the day, my love," he answered pantingly.

"Of course," she replied understandingly while clutching him greedily still between her thighs. For, having received such a heavenly effusion, Natalie decided to say nothing of what she had seen, nor to give any hint as to her knowledge of the affair. From then on, however, she became more watchful.

Susan for her part, though, became ever more devious, and frequently joined her stepfather in the summer house or some other discreet rendezvous. He rapidly introduced her to all the amorous arts, inducing her to imbibe his ejaculate by way of her pretty lips and her rosy bottom hole, as well as her cunt. By then Susan was in such a glow of health that her mother renewed her suspicions, for the winsome girl had become positively smug and would frequently give her papa the most amorous looks when she thought they were not observed. Soon enough, as must occur in all such matters, carelessness intruded.

Having ensured that the couple found no opportunity whatever for their illicit passions, Natalie put her vigorously equipped husband to such frustration that he was mindful to find cause to give Susan another strapping, which intent he thought it frightfully clever to avow openly.

Playing her part as well as she could, Susan sobbed and protested to no avail, as well she hoped, since she had been deprived of a lusty ramming for several weeks.

"Why, Susan, you must obey your dear papa at all times," declared Natalie, who was then careful to add that she intended to retire, which of course delighted both her husband and daughter, though they were careful not to show it. "I am tired, my dear, so you must forgive me. Apply the strap to the naughty girl's bottom well, for I am sure she stands in need of it." She then made great play of retiring to her boudoir and closing the door.

Albeit that her heart was beating rapidly, Natalie allowed quite some minutes for passions to reach their heights and endeavored to distract herself by disrobing to her corset and stockings and casting on a chiffon peignoir. She had now every intention of interrupting the pair, though in truth she was not yet sure of what she was going to do upon effecting her surprise entry.

She listened for several minutes to the regular smacking of the strap and the plaintive cries and moans of Susan, which Natalie knew well enough by now how to interpret. With her pulse racing and her palms more than a little moist, Natalie then moved quietly along the corridor in the direction of the study and silently opened the door.

Susan at first neither heard nor saw her, for she was in the very throes of pleasure. Her dress, chemise, and drawers, were strewn upon the floor, along with the little-used strap. Nearby, her stepfather's garments also adorned the carpet, together with his boots. Naked as the day, he knelt upon the divan with his stiff prick half inserted in the moist nest of his stepdaughter who, on hands and knees before him, looked divinely desirable in her white silk stockings, pink garters, and nothing else save for her boots. At that very moment, her papa's cock was entering her again after several juicy thrusts, which had already churned their bellies warmly. Bent over her, his palms fervently cupped her breasts, whose creamy, swollen surfaces offered the tingling of her aroused nipples to his touch.

Murmuring incoherently but blissfully, Susan kept her flushed face resting on her forearms while moving her hips about gently as he had taught her to. Reaching his free arm under her smooth tummy, her papa caused his fingers to toy around her clitoris while his cock moved powerfully in and out between the greedily sucking walls of her cunt. Lubricated as it was by her secretions, for Susan had already come once even as he had inserted his bulbous knob in her. his prick moved easily. Albeit that she was blissfully tight, she had learned rapidly how to apply the nutcracker action of her interior muscles to draw him on.

Natalie stood silently swaying in the doorway, holding onto the door frame as she gazed upon this erotic spectacle until, suddenly becoming aware of her presence, Susan uttered a wild cry.

Sir Eustace, who at this point was so close to release that he was only motivated by desire, seized Susan's waggling hips and rammed his charger full into her so that her heated bottom cheeks balled tightly into his belly. Then, reaching out with his right arm, he seized his wife's wrist and he pulled her down beside them.

"Ah, Eustace no," Natalie cried out, finding her face adjacent to her daughter's while her robe was manually thrust open and her own cunt offered to her husband's hand.

"Oh yes, Natalie," he told her, determined not to be deprived of his final pleasure in this ardent moment and, indeed, to add to it. His wife's sturdy, black-stockinged legs, kicking wildly, contrasted erotically with the white ones of Susan, who could do nothing but moan as his instrument continued to pound her. All was then lost in the wild passion of the moment. Torn between outrage and arising passion, Natalie succumbed, knowing full well that she had no other course to take anyway, other than to totally disrupt the very relations that ensured her steady supply of caviar and champagne. Thus did opportunism reign.

Continuing to soak his pestle into Susan, who by then lay flat beneath him,

Sir Eustace afforded his wife the most passionate of kisses and continued to caress her own pulpy slit. In this manner all three ran a delirious course to completion, after which they settled into a softly breathing quiet.

"Oh, Eustace, what are we at?" Natalie finally murmured.

"Naught but pleasure, my pet, and who is to say us nay? But come, let us all to the boudoir where we may have a larger bed on which to spread ourselves." Then, withdrawing then his still-thick penis from his daughter's come-soaked nest, he eased mother and daughter to their trembling legs.

"Oh, Mama, what are we to do? I cannot," Susan wailed, covering her blushing face.

"What nonsense, Susan, you have done it with Papa once and you might as well do it again," declared Natalie rather to her own surprise.

Swept up in her stepfather's arms, Susan was then carried to the bed, kicking and sobbing theatrically, as she felt it necessary to do. In this, Natalie saw well enough her opportunity for some revenge at least. She persuaded her husband to spank the wicked girl soundly in their bedroom until, if not quieted, she was at least sufficiently subdued. A session she found most enjoyable to watch.

Sir Eustace then ordered both mother and daughter to dutifully fondle his thoroughly re-aroused cock before threading them both in turn. Much to their shameful delight, each of them was forced to witness the other in the throes of desire. By morning, Natalie had been thrice pumped and Susan twice more, so that each fully received their due.

NOT WISHING TO LET her daughter take an upper hand in the matter, Natalie thereafter saw to it that when Susan received her papa's cock it was always in her presence, often after he had spanked his stepdaughter to Natalie's delight. It was a strange but knowing relationship that then existed between Susan and her mother, one which Natalie contrived to successfully use to her advantage after Sir Eustace suffered a heart attack and died two months later.

Chapter Two: The Plan

While Natalie was left an allowance following the death of her husband, the majority of the estate went to his son, who required Natalie and Susan to depart from the main house since he intended to live there. He did permit them to stay in the London townhouse for as long as they wished to, however, but they had no ownership over it.

Natalie fretted that she could no longer afford to visit boutiques and tea houses, but there remained one diversion she could still partake of which had become a very important part of her life. Namely her penchant for the rod, which she considered to be one of the most voluptuous and delicious institutions of private life and which she was sorely missing following Sir Eustace's demise. She and other ladies who were of like mind met monthly at a ladies club, created by Anna Quinlan, known to gentlemen as Madame Q, exclusively for female admirers of birching. The meetings were held in a special room on one of the upper floors of Anna's house, also known as The Nunnery.

The income that Natalie received from her late husband's estate would have kept many in bread, cheese, beef, and wine for a lifetime, but she refused to even consider the life of a regular person. These were people whom she looked down upon as if they were an entirely different species. Moreover, Susan was an additional weight upon her, for her daughter also sought to continue the same comforts she had always known, and had seemingly no idea where money actually came from. Unless something changed soon, there would be no more caviar and champagne, no more hunting and shooting parties, and no more mingling with other aristocratic ladies. No, Natalie was a lady who had always lived life well, and she was determined to do whatever it might take to prevent life's riches from slipping away from her. She knew she had to act swiftly, before her loss of status became widely known which would cause her to be excluded from high society. Natalie reasoned that her only option would be to search for a third husband. One who would not so much be a breadwinner, nor even a bread-and-cheese winner, but a caviar supplier and a diamond provider. So, since Anna Quinlan was so well connected, Natalie took her aside after the next club meeting and asked if she could take Anna into her confidence.

"Of course, it would be my pleasure," Anna told her, acknowledging that Natalie was clearly vexed. "But let us adjourn to the lounge where we might chat more comfortably over tea."

Natalie explained to Anna, that following the death of her husband, she now could only reside in the townhouse and had been reduced to an allowance which was by no means sufficient to support her former lifestyle.

"And you seek a wealthy husband to restore you, then." Anna nodded, pouring out two cups of tea as she spoke.

"Precisely." Natalie responded. "Preferably an older gentleman, for I do understand that being close to forty years old would make me unsuitable for most men in search of a wife. However, I am most adept at running a substantial household and would gladly take that burden upon myself."

"Tell me of your sex life, Natalie." Anna queried without inflection. "Would you call yourself active? Enthusiastic?"

"Oh, more than you might imagine." Suddenly remembering that she was speaking to the Madame of The Nunnery, Natalie's face blushed crimson. "I mean, um, Lord Eustace enjoyed me, and, um, others, in a variety of ways."

"Others?" Anna coaxed. "And you were privy to this?"

Both of Natalie's hands went to her mouth.

"Pray tell. I must know all if I am to be assistance to you."

"I, on occasion, would procure services from one of the maids," Natalie's blushing continued. "And then watch him with them." She took a deep breath and sat up straight. "This would serve as a most arousing foreplay for us."

"I see." Anna said approvingly. "As a member of our club I know you be an adventurous lady, and the fact you are uninhibited sexually certainly puts you in good stead as you endeavor to find a new partner." She refilled their tea cups. "But have you considered that also qualifies you to achieve your financial goals right away." Anna's eyes sparkled at Natalie's confusion. "There are a number of gentlemen who visit this house who would find time with you most desirable. This would provide an immediate solution to your current financial situation." She shrugged. "And you could take time in your search for a husband, if you still wished for matrimony. In fact, you may even find one here."

Natalie was stunned. "I, I never imagined..." she began.

"Perhaps not consciously, Natalie. But, you must admit my solution does address your most immediate concern. You also may not realize that several of the ladies who reside here enjoy an active social life as escorts to ranking gentlemen, and as such attend some of the most prestigious events in London." She chuckled. "In fact, you probably already know some of them." She sat back. "So tell me, do you have any current spousal prospects in your sights?"

"Actually, yes. There is one. A close friend of my late husband sent me a delightful letter of condolence and offered any assistance that he may be able to provide. He is joining me for tea tomorrow."

"Splendid! What's his name?"

"He is a doctor. His name is Archibald Onan." Natalie watched Anna's expression. "You know him?"

"I do, indeed. Very well, in fact." Anna grinned and slowly shook her head. "Dr. Onan is the house doctor here at The Nunnery." She looked directly at Natalie. "He is a most confirmed bachelor, you know."

"Perhaps. But I'm also aware of certain proclivities he favors. I often listened at the keyhole in our old drawing room while he and Sir Eustace enjoyed after dinner drinks and cigars."

"Oh? And do you have the means to appeal to his eccentricities?"

"Not personally, for he enjoys such trysts with younger women. No, I intend to entice him with a potential stepdaughter. My eighteen year old Susan."

"Really?" Anna stroked her chin. "What does Susan have to say about being used as bait?"

"She will have no problem with it. You see, she and her former stepfather used to enjoy each other in much the same manner. She is likely an erotomaniac, and has since confessed to me that she is excited by older men."

"And you had no objections to her dalliances with your husband?"

"Why should I? I actually believe it was Susan who initiated all that to begin with." Natalie looked right at Anna. "I've never told this to another soul, but after I discovered them together, Sir Eustace used to have us both at the same time. So, as you can see, I certainly would not stand to interfere with any of Dr. Onan's desires should he agree to marry me."

Anna nodded thoughtfully. She knew Dr. Onan well enough to know that he would not fall victim to Natalie's plans, but that result would be of benefit to her as Madame Q. Natalie would, no doubt, be a splendid addition to The Nunnery, but her daughter, Susan, sounded particularly intriguing. A resident, educated lady convincingly portraying a young, innocent-yet-naughty girl would find herself much in demand.

SINCE DR. ONAN HAD been one of her husband's best friends, Natalie and he were well acquainted with each other, and his wealth and standing in society had always impressed her even more than his handsome appearance. So, in spite of Anna Quinlan's warning that the doctor was a confirmed bachelor, Natalie nevertheless intended to pursue him as a potential husband. Herein laid the opportunity to better her circumstances while also maintaining her daughter's, upon whom she had high hopes in order to bring her plan to fruition.

Clearly, such hopes were not of the high moralistic nature that one might have hoped for a lady of her standing. Susan was to seduce Dr. Onan, thus providing the eventual lure that would draw him into the center of Natalie's web. Natalie, therefore, made few bones about the matter when broaching the plan to her daughter. Since Susan knew well enough what was afoot, Natalie declared her intentions regarding Dr. Onan quite boldly. "You will be very nice to him, Susan. Very nice! Do you understand?"

"Oh, yes, Mama. I do." Susan smirked. "If he should wish to kiss me, you mean?"

"Yes, that's correct."

"And, Mama, if he should wish to..."

"Tut, tut, Susan, there are certain things we need not discuss. Should Dr. Onan find it necessary to, um, want to spank you, as your dear papa was wont to do, then naturally I shall raise no objections."

"But, Mama, he may wish to strap me, and, oh, dear, if he does so I shall have to take my drawers down." She giggled teasingly.

"I do not doubt it, my dear, but that is a problem which has caused you little concern in the past and need not do so now. The better that you present your bottom, the more engaging will be his interest."

With that, neither could suppress a laugh. They both had fond memories of all that had passed and were as lewd in their minds as ever they had been.

Dr. Onan arrived promptly for tea and was shown into the lounge where Natalie and Susan were eagerly awaiting his arrival. Natalie was wearing a black gown which, while appropriate in color for a widow, nevertheless displayed an ample portion of her breasts. "Thank you so much for your kind letter of condolence, Dr. Onan," she cooed. "You remember Susan? See how pretty she has become?"

"Indeed," Dr. Onan responded politely. "It is my pleasure to see you both again."

"Don't you think her dress suits her admirably, for it shows off some of her best attributes?"

Dr. Onan's eyes drank in the curves which were accentuated by the clinging of Susan's pretty blue dress. "You are a most charming young lady, Susan." Dr. Onan nodded politely as he spoke.

"Of course, it may perhaps be trifle daring" Natalie continued as she poured the tea and handed the doctor a china cup and saucer. "But I believe a girl should have no concerns displaying herself while at home. We are all perhaps too modest in our ways, do you not think?"

"Ah, Lady Smithers, you are indeed bold. But," he changed the subject. "Tell me, how are you both faring? Are you both able to continue living in London?"

"Oh, indeed we are quite well, thank you," Natalie replied.

That her guest did not rejoice more in the ample offerings of both Susan's and her curves fretted Natalie. Neither did Dr. Onan appear affected by their openly flirtatious mannerisms. In fact, it was if he were actually immune to them, along with the innuendo she cloaked in the most discreet of conversation as is proper amongst polite society. Based on the manner in which he swayed any conversation away from the directions Natalie intended, she was forced to conclude that while Dr. Onan possessed the monetary wealth she required, he lacked any interest in pursuing a matrimonial bond. Unfortunately, he was the only prospect Natalie had.

"So, what will we do now?" Susan asked after Dr. Onan had left.

"Susan, my dear." Natalie suddenly brightened up. "I am going to introduce you to a friend of mine who promises an immediate solution for both of us." She grinned at Susan's confusion. "Her name is Anna Quinlan."

Chapter Three: An Older Gentleman

The honorable Reginald Mane gazed somberly about his study. He often thought about tidying it up, but he rather enjoyed its familiar disorder of so never acted on those thoughts. None of his servants were permitted to enter this particular domain, for within it he guarded secrets that were to be seen by no eyes other than his own. In his duties as a Member of Parliament, he was naturally privy to papers of a confidential nature that even his departed wife had never gazed upon. More importantly for him, she had certainly never settled her eyes upon a most interesting collection of books, which he had acquired during his various visits into London. Such erotic delicacies, enlivened as some were by colored plates, amused him from time to time.

But like many secret seekers of pleasure, Reginald Mane could never quite obtain what he most wanted, despite his urgent seeking among the shelves of bookshops of ill repute. For while these books had sustained him throughout his marriage, he now hungered for experiences he had never enjoyed since his late youth. More than voyeurism, he fondly remembered that it was actually the control he once exerted over a woman that aroused him so. Furthermore, even though he found it hard to confess to himself, it was the wanton domination of a submissive woman that aroused him most of all. To have her raise her skirts on command and obey his every whim.

He had first been introduced to such activities by Lady Christina Hardcastle of the local manor. This was during his college days when he had been enjoying a summer holiday on his family estate by upping the skirts of several farm girls. The young Reginald had fondled their cunts, caressed their naked bottoms, and given himself many an erection thereby. Curiously, he had sought not to fuck them, but rather to observe such underwear as they wore and to thrill to the shapeliness of the bottoms and thighs that the raising of their skirts revealed. Though his cock stirred up well during these activities, it did not then present the proud proportions that, unknown to Reginald at the time, it was soon to do.

It was in such a moment, close to one of the cowsheds, that Lady Christina had come upon him feasting his eyes upon the quim of a young woman, whom he had paid five shillings to see. The farm girl, shrieking, ran off, while Reginald stood hot-cheeked in the face of discovery.

Lady Christina was wearing a black riding outfit and carrying, somewhat menacingly as it seemed to him, a silver-handled crop. Expecting her to upbraid him then and there, his momentary relief dwindled into apprehension when he was told briefly to follow her to her house.

Walking a few paces behind her gave Reginald an opportunity to observe the rolling of the lady's bottom cheeks, which were rather closely sheathed by her skirt, fashionably designed to pay homage to her posterior. He delighted in watching those firm hemispheres, displaying themselves so boldly with each sway of her hips, and he began to fantasize about somehow coercing her to raise her skirt up for him. Consequently, Reginald's cock was well up and prodding through his trousers upon entry to the house, where he was led silently up to Lady Christina's boudoir.

Without expression, she ordered him to stand still while she removed her gloves and hat, then took up the crop again in a manner that made Reginald swallow hard. "I see I have your full attention," she told him as she licked her lips. "You are a gentleman, sir," she admonished. "And, as such, should not be pursuing the grubby chemises and mud-spattered bottoms of farm girls. It is therefore incumbent upon me to administer a correction to your behavior."

Finding no words to excuse himself, Reginald could say nothing and only wonder what was to happen next. He was not kept in this state of ignorance for long.

"Turn about now, sir, and kneel," she commanded, standing majestically above him as he acceded to the humble position.

Lady Christina then proceeded to draw up her black pleated skirt, enabling his bemused and heated eyes to fall on the full majesty of her long, ivory legs. He scarcely had time to absorb this pulse-beating view before the skirt descended over his head, enveloping him in darkness. Covered right down to his buttocks by the long fall of her skirt, his ears were trapped between her thighs. Reginald's senses reeled as the crotch of her silk drawers brushed his nose. No words being uttered, Lady Christina then placed her hand over the bulge of his head and pushed upwards, ramming Reginald's mouth against her silk-sheathed cunt. Pushing his mouth in farther, he felt his lips splurge against those of her slit through the thin material.

Reginald grew heady and dizzy while relishing in the joy of what he was now doing. He was in a veritable haven of delights, of fresh linen, of sheer silk stockings, and of a soft, spotless chemise that fell about his face as did her skirt. He began to amorously lick until he felt her firm bottom quiver, the cheeks tightening as a spasm shook her and her fine, salty rain of pleasure filtered slowly through the silk to ooze upon his tongue.

After a few silent moments Lady Christina again raised her skirt, releasing Reginald who almost fell backwards as he blinked into the daylight.

"Up with you now." Lady Christina smiled at the prominent bulge in front of Reginald's pants as she spoke. "I must insist that it is now time for you to remove your boots, your socks, and your trousers, sir."

Reginald was still in such a dither that he almost mindlessly followed her recommendation, and in short order presented his upstanding penis to her gaze with a mingled mixture of embarrassment and excitement. His most virile possession now totally on show, Lady Christina took it into her right hand and began to fondle it. Then, without taking her eyes off this prize, she eased to her knees in front of him. "I now wish to pleasure you, sir," she said, continuing her examination of his erect cock until she could resist no more and slid her parted lips across the bulbous head, taking him into her warm mouth. Stimulating the underside of his member with her tongue, she began slowly rocking back and forth while closing her mouth around it. He exploded furiously into it the instant she began to suck.

Easing back, her eyes looked up. "Reginald, will you do a favor for me?" She asked sweetly.

"Anything you wish, my lady," he responded, offering his hands to help her to her feet.

"I want you to spank my bottom, and while you do I wish to make myself come with a dildo."

"Then prepare yourself, my lady," Reginald's cock began to restore as he spoke. "For I should like nothing more than to spank your buttocks."

Lady Christina crossed to the other side of the room and opened a drawer from which she removed a dildo. Then, standing in front of him, she divested herself of everything except her corset, stockings, and boots, presenting to Reginald's gaze a figure of statuesque glory. The glimpses he had up to now had of girl's bottoms, cunts, and thighs were nothing compared to the mature, ripe curves the lady was presenting to him. Her slit, being particularly hairy, had a bush that sprouted boldly upon the plump curving of her mound while her pale breasts, adorned with two ruby nipples, jiggled like blancmanges. Having already experienced the clamping of her thighs, Reginald knew their majestic fullness well, the rich creamy columns flowing up on their outer surfaces to blend into the firm rump of her bottom and the flowing of her hips. He watched excitedly as Lady Christina then silently placed herself on her hands and knees on the sofa, elevating her bottom enticingly in the air for him.

Reginald began tentatively, tapping softly rather than hard spanking her bottom, while the lady slid the dildo gently into her cunt. "Harder, spank my bottom harder," she panted.

He responded eagerly, turning her skin to a rosy hue as she twisted and wriggled under this delectable excitement. Reginald increased the intensity to provide an even, glowing patina on her buttocks while the tempo of the dildo in and out of her slit grew ever faster. The sight of her naked bottom, reddened even more with each stroke he provided, inflamed Reginald's member to the point of rigidity and it now pointed prominently out in front of him. On seeing this from the corner of her eye, Lady Christina withdrew the dildo and murmured, "Fuck me." Her voice was half begging and half ordering. "Fuck me from behind."

Needing no further encouragement, Reginald quickly knelt behind her. Approaching her thus from the rear caused an involuntary gasp to escape from the lady's lips upon feeling his engorged bulb brushing against her labia. He then thrust his hips forward to engage his cock deep into her slit that way. Then, overwhelmed with lust, he grabbed her hips and began to pound into her, delighting in this position as her bottom cheeks smacked audibly against his belly.

Following this episode, Reginald returned to the manor weekly for the rest of his holiday. While Lady Christina had initially appeared dominating to the point of almost scary, she had revealed to him her desire to be possessed and helped to develop in him his desire to have women under his control. Thus did he enjoy some momentously splendid fucks, taking her both in front and from behind. Lady Christina also introduced him to bondage, and several times had him tie her to the bed. When she was tied spreadeagled on her back he would bring her to orgasm using his fingers and mouth. And when he tied her face down he would either spank her, or sometimes flog her buttocks and the inside of her thighs before using a short-tailed leather flogger on her parted pussy lips until she begged him for release.

It also pleased him greatly that, while she was submissive to him, Lady Christina enjoyed dominating females, and on occasion she included him in her play with them. Amongst her female submissives were two of the prettiest farm girls, girls whom he had previously lusted over but who had never let him raise their skirts. Now, not only was he able to view their delicious bodies, but he also freely fucked their pussies and mouths.

It was during this summer of delight that Reginald came to the realization that women who desired sexual submission were nature's most glorious creatures. This, however, was something that he had never been able to convey to his departed wife.

Alas, Reginald sighed in his recollection that he had not been able to engage with Lady Christina for longer, for he would have learned more of the secret ways of the world. After that summer he returned to Europe to finish his studies. Then, back in England, his career rapidly ascended and he dutifully followed his father's advice to marry. He soon became a member of parliament, and following the death of his parents became master of his own house.

He had buried himself in his duties all these years since, but on becoming a widower his desire for a submissive woman began to occupy his thoughts more and more. Now matrimonially unencumbered, he yearned to return to such a world, and he found himself frequently distracted by merry tales of birching and taunted by his desire to dominate a woman for his pleasure. He fretted much that the licentious volumes he obtained gave him no guidance on how he might obtain such pleasures himself.

He found himself lusting after the females in his house staff, even though it seemed that they inhabited a different world. He wondered what might happen if he birched or spanked them, although in reality he could not imagine such a thing, for doing so seemed contrary to his position in the household. All the same, at other moments he longed to see beneath their skirts, particularly those of the upstairs maid, Patty, who was nigh on nineteen and as fulsome and curvaceous of form as any man could wish. Long had his eyes dwelt furtively on the slenderness of her waist, the promising curves of her hips, the protrusion of her breasts, and the impudent thrust of her bottom. Whenever he saw her it made his cock stir guiltily, but it was also that guilt which prohibited him from engaging in more than fantasy.

Reginald was, of course, aware of the availability of women of pleasure in the city, but as a member of parliament he was more concerned about his need for discretion to consider such folly. However, while relaxing with a second snifter of brandy at The Sagamore Club one evening, he happened to engage in conversation about the matter with Dr. Onan, who promptly arranged an interview for him with Madame Q.

Chapter Four: Mother and Daughter

"I have a request for a scenario for which the two of you are uniquely qualified," Anna began as she sat in the lounge with Natalie and Susan. They had both recently joined The Nunnery as ladies of pleasure. Natalie was developing into something of a disciplinarian, while Susan had particularly taken to entertaining gentlemen as a sweet innocent, for being paid to indulge in her erotomania with them was an ideal world for her. "An older gentleman wishes for a woman to encourage a girl to arouse him prior to satisfying him sexually," she explained. "I asked him if a mother and daughter role play might be of interest, and he is most enthusiastic about it."

"What would we be required to do?" Natalie asked.

"He has a voyeuristic desire and likes the appeal of an innocent." Madame Q winked at Susan. "Natalie will therefore instruct Susan to raise her skirts, sans drawers, so he might first look at, and then touch her. She will be shy and embarrassed, but mother," Anna nodded to Natalie, "Will press her on."

"That sounds very erotic," Susan chimed in. "Will I be able to have sex?"

"Oh yes."

Natalie and her daughter imbibed not a little wine in order to prepare themselves for the event, for both had a great taste for fine wines. They were seated side by side on the divan when

Madame Q and Reginald Mane entered their room. After making introductions, Madame Q left and Natalie invited Reginald to sit between mother and daughter. She arranged herself on one side of Reginald while Susan herself perched on the other. "You have not been a naughty girl today, have you, Susan?" Natalie asked coyly.

"Perhaps a trifle, Mama," Susan responded, her cheeks a little flushed. "But surely I shall not be disciplined for it?" She smiled at Reginald. "Perhaps if I do other things for him it would make him feel more lenient?"

Quite amazed, Reginald listened to these brief discourses while being unable to prevent his eyes from roaming occasionally over the twin melons of resilient flesh that the low-cut front of Susan's gown revealed. They were as enticing a pair as ever he had seen and served to increase his desire to look up the skirts of such a fetching young lady. To have her pose for him would be perfect.

"Her papa had to discipline her regularly, you know," Natalie explained, laying her hand on his thigh quite close to a certain prominence that had arisen in his trousers.

"Yes, he did," Susan added with a pretended pout. "And he took my drawers down and made me hold my dress up to my waist. I had to turn all about in front of him while he lectured me most severely. Oh, mama."

"Yes, dear?" Inquired Natalie, who had rehearsed this moment with Susan thoroughly while that they had been tippling earlier.

"It embarrasses me just to mention having to do such things." Then, making much ado of being shy, Susan turned and buried her face in Reginald's shoulder, so permitting him an even deeper view of the delicious chasm between her breasts. Indeed, one of her perky brown nipples rose to his view from out of the confines of her dress even as she spoke. Conical in shape and seemingly ever erect, it looked most enticing and caused his prick to quiver even more.

"M... M... Mama," Susan continued. "Papa would make me stand in front of him with my dress held up and he would pat my bottom with one hand and t... t... tickle me in front with the other."

'That, my pet, was merely to make you pay attention. Do you not concur, Reginald?" Natalie passed her hand lightly but boldly over his penis, which by now was threatening to burst his trousers, causing Susan to giggle and to press her lips as though by accident to the side of his neck.

"Ah, yes, perhaps, indeed," Reginald stammered in response.

"Mama, I always wriggled when Papa tickled me so," Susan murmured, passing the tip of her tongue between her lips so that it tickled Ralph in turn and made him feel quite dizzy.

"Of course, Susan, it is fitting that a young lady should do that in the private presence of her Papa. It were better perhaps that he had taken your drawers off completely that you might present a better posture for his pleasure."

"Oh, he did, Mama, frequently, though I would blush exceedingly for his hands would then pass of necessity all about my bottom and thighs. I would clutch at him in my shyness while he then divested me of my gown and chemise, for he ever insisted that I need wear nothing but my stockings and boots for chastisement."

"Oh," Reginald exclaimed at this juncture, squirming slightly. By devious manipulations of her fingers, Natalie had succeeded in loosening three of the front buttons of his trousers.

She then passed her fingers over his stemming cock beneath, though her movements were so gentle and subtle that all seemed to be happening most naturally.

"Well, my dear," Natalie continued speaking to Susan. "To be taught to present yourself properly is fundamental to a young lady's deportment. Do you not think so, Reginald?"

"Um, yes, absolutely." Reginald responded, quite flushed with excitement.

"And since we have determined that Susan has been a naughty girl, you must also agree that she be disciplined forthwith." Natalie then addressed her daughter. "In the absence of a papa being available, we will need to ask Mr. Mane here if he will be so kind as to provide you with your discipline."

"I am sure that Mr. Mane is a kindly man and would not wish to sting my poor bottom if I behaved properly for him now." Susan pretended a pout.

Natalie leaned forward and whispered, "Would you like that?" Into Reginald's ear. "I will ensure that she properly thanks you following."

While Reginald stumbled for a response, Natalie leaned back. "Stand up, Susan," she instructed. "And show us how well you were taught, so Mr. Mane may have knowledge of your aptitudes in disciplinary matters."

Susan obediently rose from the seat on which the three were huddled and, turning about, slowly raised her skirts to offer closely to his view as perfect a pair of bottom cheeks as Reginald had ever seen. Natalie then released his upstanding prick fully and massaged it gently in her grasp.

The effect upon Reginald was naturally electric.

Susan then bent over and dipped her back so that not only her proud nether cheeks but also the fig of her cunt were presented to his heated gaze.

Passing her fingers down under his throbbing tool and feeling for his balls, Natalie drew them out in turn and cradled them lovingly on her palm. "What think you, Reginald," she purred. "Is that not the most delightful bottom you have ever seen? Feel how smooth it is."

Reginald reached out with both hands to massage Susan's lovely cream cheeks.

"This naughty girl drove her papa to distraction, I do believe. Move back a little closer, Susan. Let Mr. Mane see how you have been well taught to show yourself."

Susan artfully brought the backs of her knees to touch Reginald and thereby presented her now parted cunt for his up close examination. "Splendidly formed, is she not?" Natalie whispered rhetorically while her hand on Reginald's member grew ever more persuasive as his fingers slid between Susan's labia lips. She wriggled against them until they contacted her aroused clitoris. "More, please," she moaned. "Please, sir. Please frig me to completion."

So encouraged, Reginald vibrated his thumb on her clitoris while slipping two fingers into her soaked vagina while Natalie continued her slow stimulation of his cock.

Suddenly, Susan emitted a gasp and her knees began to buckle, but she caught herself before she actually stumbled. Natalie leaned onto Reginald's shoulder. "She often had cause to sit upon her papa's lap for comforting after such activity," she told him. Then, addressing her daughter again, "Did you not, Susan?

Come, be truthful, girl, for I am sure that Mr. Mane would wish you to be so."

"Yes, Mama. After I was a little naughty by letting papa see me and touch me like that," Susan uttered in trembling tone. "I would have to sit on his lap."

"Perhaps Mr. Mane would like you to demonstrate?"

"I used to sit upon papa's p...p...p... LAP... like this," she panted, accompanying her words with actions. To the throbbing joy of Reginald, Susan positioned herself upon him so that his stout penis, which Natalie quickly released, stuck lewdly up between the tops of her thighs and poked its purplish head enquiringly against her wanting cunt.

Reginald took hold of her hips as she lowered herself in order to properly ease himself fully into her. She then rocked back and forth, which after only a few minutes caused him to jerk and moan with pleasure. Then, when it became clear that he was approaching climax, Susan slid off his lap onto the floor, pushed his thighs apart, and quickly positioned herself on her knees between them. Her head went forward and she took his entire glistening cock deep into her mouth, whereupon Reginald instantly achieved the most plentiful ejaculation that he had experienced in years.

Chapter Five: Spanking Susan

"Was your time with Susan and her mother to your liking, Mr. Mane?" Madame Q asked.

"Oh, very much so." Reginald was beaming. "In fact, I would like another scene, but this time just with Susan, for she is such a charming creature. I want her to continue as a shy, innocent girl who has been naughty and is in need of a sound spanking. A spanking I wish to deliver upon her most delightful posterior."

"And sex acts afterwards?"

"Well," Reginald twisted his mouth and looked askance.

"There is no need for embarrassment, Mr. Mane." Madame Q smiled and touched his knee with her left hand. "The Nunnery is a unique vehicle for clients to both freely express all of their desires and then subsequently experience them. And always with complete discretion and without judgment."

Reginald looked directly at her. "I would very much desire to also bugger her?" His face reddened. "For it is something I've always wanted to try..."

"With a shy innocent girl." Madame Q completed his words and smiled. "But, of course. Do you have a thought on how you would like her dressed for you?"

"Is it possible for her to be wearing something both innocent and yet provocative at the same time?" He asked excitedly.

"Most certainly, my dear Mr. Mane," Madame Q responded. "She will present just as you wish." She smiled again. Madame Q had already learned enough about Reginald Mane to know precisely what he would like to see. "I have the perfect outfit for her in mind."

Madame Q did not disappoint. Susan presented in a pastel blue dress adorned with ribbons and lace, and with ribbons in her blonde hair she was positively angelic from the waist up. The skirt, however, while of the same composition, was so short that almost the entire length of her legs were on naked display. Reginald sat in an armchair for a full ten minutes while she stood in front of him, turning from one side to another while posing at his command, feigning shyness and remaining compliantly still when he lifted up her short skirt to reveal nothing beneath it.

"It is a naughty girl, indeed, who goes about without drawers, is it not, Susan?" Reginald asked.

"Yes, sir." She responded demurely. "I confess, I have been a naughty girl." She looked up sheepishly. "What must be done with me?"

"I shall be required to spank your bottom." He stood up, put his right arm around her, and walked her across the room. "Come," he said. "Bend over the arm of the settee."

Susan settled her midriff across the padded arm and placed her hands flat on the couch cushion. Her bottom half showed under the short skirt, but Reginald eagerly raised it and laid it across her back. Thus positioned, her buttocks were now displayed perfectly with the coral lips of her cunt peeking out of their nest of fine curls between her thighs. "Spread your legs a little further apart," Reginald instructed, then slid the fingers of his right hand against her slit as she complied. He spread her labia lips apart and, locating her clitoris, teased it with his forefinger.

"Oh, Mr. Mane," Susan cooed. "That feels so wonderful."

Reginald eased his hand away and caressed her buttocks before standing to her left side. "I shall now provide you with your spanking," he told her.

Susan jerked forward slightly and she uttered a faint yelp as Reginald brought the flat of his right hand hard across her bottom. It made an extremely satisfying sound, and he quickly followed it with another, then a third. A rouge glow began to appear on her bottom cheeks as he continued, and soon her bottom was brought to a delightful patina as Susan panted, but remained obediently still. Reginald then slid his fingers again between her legs. Clearly, Susan was thoroughly enjoying the sensations she was being afforded for she was now heavily lubricated. "Please, sir," she gasped. "Please do not spank me further. I promise to be a good girl for you."

"What does it mean to be a good girl?" Reginald's prick was pushing against the inside of his trousers.

"I will do anything you want, sir." She turned her head to face him. "Anything at all."

Reginald could contain himself no longer. Unbuttoning his trousers, he quickly stood Susan up and then placed her on her knees on the floor before him while he released his member. Then, taking her left hand he forced her to feel his standing cock. "You have such a pretty mouth," he told her. "That I shall have you use it to pleasure me."

"Yes, sir," Susan replied while sliding her hand up and down his rigid rod. "Like this?"

Reginald gasped as Susan sucked several inches of his tool into her mouth while continuing to stimulate it with her hand. He grabbed her head, thrusting himself deeper and deeper, in and out. He had planned to desist prior to completion in order to save his ejaculate for another entrance, but the actions of Susan's tongue combined with the fact he was actually fucking this beautiful girl's face caused him to lose control, and he soon bathed the inside of her mouth with his hot semen.

He remained in this position while she continued to suck, then after she had swallowed the last drop he slowly removed himself from between her lips.

"Was I a good girl?" She asked sweetly.

"Oh, you are a very good girl. And now I want you to bend over the settee arm again," he told her. His trousers were now around his ankles and he kicked them away before positioning himself behind her.

"Shall I spread my legs again for you?" Susan asked in a whisper.

"Indeed, yes, my girl, for I desire a full view of and access to your pussy." His fingers slipped between her labia lips and he teased her now engorged clitoris. "What a sweet little slit you have," he complimented her. "What silky down adorns it, and how it responds so delightfully to my caresses."

"Oh, oh," Susan moaned. "Are you going to fuck me, sir?"

"I am indeed, my dear," Reginald responded. His excitement at what he was about to do had not only restored his cock, but it was now even more erect than before. "But I do not mean to fuck your pussy," he continued as his fingers began to anoint her tight little bottom hole with her own juices. "Now, keep your legs apart and push your bottom out," he ordered as he spread her buttocks apart and positioned his purple bulb against her puckered orifice.

He fully inserted the head of his cock in a single move, then remained still until her sphincter settled down. As the muscle gradually relaxed, he eased himself further inside before reaching around her with his right hand to frig her in front. Susan became wild, screaming with delight as she spent over Reginald's fingers before her body became compliantly limp. With this, Reginald pushed his prick forward until it became fully engulfed up her bottom. He took her hips in his hands and slid half way out, waited a moment, then slammed back into her. Proceeding then to fuck her this way with rapturous in and out movements, he entered into the greatest pitch of excitement he had ever known. Even after ejaculating into her, Susan's anal muscles massaging his cock enabled him to do so again before he finally withdrew, during which time she also came twice again.

Reginald Mane now visits Susan at The Nunnery at least monthly, and she has also become quite the favorite amongst those gentlemen who enjoy her convincingly innocent demeanor. For her part, Susan delights in being paid to indulge in her favorite activities with these older men.

THE END

About the Author

With keen interest in nineteenth and early twentieth century history, Dorian Shellan writes a variety of stories with Victorian settings.

The Victorian era was one of great innovations, industrial, medical, and social. Dorian's stories incorporate many of these changes and the impact it had on the population of that time.

Dorian's genres range from novels, including adventure and romance, to short stories, to Victorian erotica.

Read more at https://victorianstories.com.